BUCKAMOO GIRLS

by Ellen A. Kelley

Illustrated by Tom Curry

Abrams Books for Young Readers
New York

The pictures in this book were made with acrylic paint on hardboard.

Designer: Chad W. Beckerman
Production Manager: Alexis Mentor

Library of Congress Cataloging-in-Publication Data:
Kelley, Ellen A.
Buckamoo girls / by Ellen A. Kelley ; illustrated by Tom Curry.
p. cm.
Summary: Rhyming text relates the adventures of two cows who
long to be cowgirls as they head to the rodeo, participate in a hoedown,
and experience other aspects of the "buckamoo girl" life.
[1. Cows—Fiction. 2. Cowgirls—Fiction. 3. Stories in rhyme.] I. Curry, Tom, ill. II. Title.

ISBN 10: 0-8109-5471-0
ISBN 13: 978-0-8109-5471-7

PZ83.C3977Buc 2006
[E]—dc22
2005022547

Printed and bound in Hong Kong
10 9 8 7 6 5 4 3 2 1

HNA
harry n. abrams, inc.
a subsidiary of La Martinière Groupe
115 West 18th Street
New York, NY 10011
www.hnabooks.com

For Evans, with special cowgirl thanks,
and in fond memory of Anita Grace Chavez

—E.A.K.

To sister Susanne
(who bears no resemblance to Susanna),
and to the memory of cousin Tedi—two buckaroo
cowgirls from west Texas who are forever inseparable

—T.C.

Two cows

out back,
spotted brown
spotted black.
Cud-munchin'
musey moos
dream of bein'

buckaroos.

Silver spurs,
  wooly vest.
Tenderhooves
  headin' West.

Saddle up,
  boots on.
Giddy-up
  and giddy-gone!

Susanna's
stirrups slide.
Prickly pear,
blister hide!

Joanna,
spurs hurt!
Horsey rears.
Hit the dirt.

Up again—that-a-way!

Now yer cowgirls, yippee-yay!

Susanna-Bandana,

Joanna-Montana.

Sit tall,
        moo strong.
Drive the herd
        now, git along!
Rumblin' river,
        tumbleweed,
sidewinder,
        stampede!

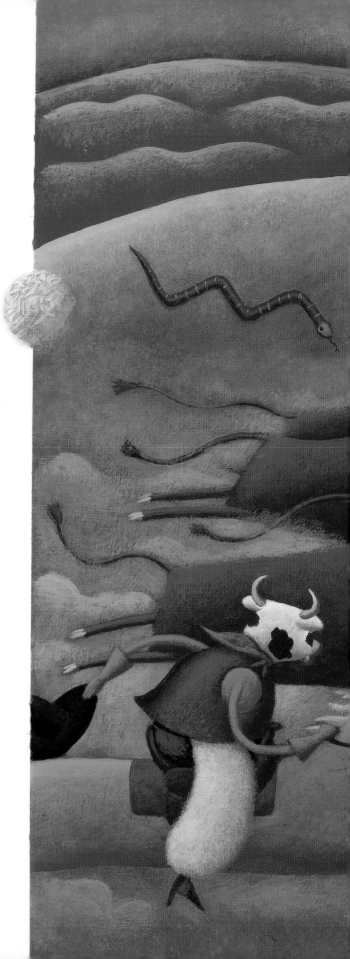

Lightning
FLASHES,

Thunder
CRACKS.

Muddy chaps,
drippy hats.

Storm's passin', head fer town,
find a fiddlin' hoe-down.
Two-step, do-si-do,
Next door . . .

Rodeo!

Lariat,
    spin 'n' ride,
ropin' calves,
    hog-tied.

Snortin' bull,
     sharp horn.
Bucked off,
     britches torn.

Plumb tuckered,
         droopy tail,
trottin' down
         the home trail.

Mighty hungry,
  won't be long.
Chuck wagon,
  dinner gong.

Clover chili,
  sweetgrass stew
smellin' fine,
  chomp 'n' chew.

Wind's up,

moon's bright.

Bunkhouse

pillow fight.

Campfire,
    strummin' tune.
Drowsy cowgirls
    sleepin' soon.

Back to pasture's
    grassy seas,
spinnin' yarns of
    cowgirl sprees.

Buckamoo Girls, won't you come out tonight, come out tonight, come out tonight? Oh, Buckamoo Girls, won't you come out tonight, and dance by the light of the MOOOOOOON?

Yer cowgirl ride
sets with the sun.
You were cowgirls
jest fer fun!